Masked Encounter

An Enemies to Lovers Romance

Bellina Acosta

Copyright © 2022 by Bellina Acosta

All rights reserved.

No portion of this book may be reproduced in any form without written permission from the publisher or author, except as permitted by U.S. copyright law.

Contents

Blurbs

♥

He fired me and ruined my career, and yet the unthinkable happened between us.

How could I be so foolish?

It was dubbed "The Ultimate White-collar Masquerade."

All the big shots were there.

And then there were the people like me.

If only I had known that beneath the mask on the dance floor... Randy Maven, the same man who ridiculed me in my job interview; the same job interview could have changed everything.

I might not have fallen for him.

I might not have made the biggest mistake in my life.

But his eyes were passionate,
His face was rough with stubble,
His charm was undeniable.
He was utterly irresistible.

But I would resist...

Chapter 1

♥

R*andy*

In a room full of people, very important people, her lips stood out to me. I needed those lips. I needed to know what they felt like. I needed them wrapped around something.

The extravagant masquerade ball was a sight to behold, with guests donning lavish masks and costumes to conceal their identities. This special event was attended by some of the most influential CEOs and staff from around the world, giving the attendees the opportunity to meet new people and interact without prejudice. The event was organized and executed by Skydeck, an organization that owned a plethora of businesses in a variety of industries, including network television, sports events, and many more. In the global marketplace, they were considered to be among the best.

The masquerade ball provided a unique outlet for guests to socialize without the pressure of having to be completely authentic. It seems people often find it difficult to be their true selves when they are around their superiors or those they aspire to be like, so the masquerade ball served as a welcome reprieve. The elegant costumes and masks provided a sense of anonymity that made it easier for guests to interact without fear of judgment or scrutiny. It was an event truly worthy of the grandeur and glamor that it deserved.

Coincidentally, I was the CEO and owner of Skydeck. I must admit: anyone who has ever worked for me has seen tremendous professional growth. That's because, despite our many different lines of business, I always kept my core team small. Thus, if Skydeck were the owner of a company, the number of people responsible for overseeing it would be small.

Even though it was my money that made the masquerade ball possible and my idea that inspired it, I still had to hire staff to make it a success. I commissioned a group to determine the guest list, to hire the caterers, to outsource the masks. That's just how things ran around here. You hire people who specialize in the tasks you need done.

Where does that leave me, then? On the outskirts, watching everything from a distance while in the thick of things. My eyes kept wandering back to this one gorgeous woman, and

I couldn't help but admit to myself that I was lusting after her. She chatted it up with a couple of strangers. However, it was unclear who else she might have been with. Frankly, I didn't want to cause any trouble for myself. In my position, flirting with anyone could end rather horridly. Those of us who live in the modern era would be terminated for such behavior. *You don't shit where you eat.*

Yet, on the other hand, she was absolutely stunning. Actually, it wasn't just her lips. I think it was her figure; perhaps it was the eyes hidden behind that mask. I wanted her to want me. To put it simply, I desired the lady.

The sight of the woman in her eye-catching, modern red dress stirred a spark of hope within me; I couldn't take my eyes off of her, and as our gazes met I knew that she had noticed me. This gave me a newfound sense of courage and confidence, and emboldened me to take action if

I wanted to make something happen. But maybe that was all in my head.

Either way, I intended to approach her. Let's see what the girl in the red dress was all about.

Chapter 2

♥

Madison

Surely he's not looking at me? Given the masks, it was obviously difficult to determine. But even with the mask on, I could tell he was attractive. That's what my instincts were telling me, at least. He was also much taller than the typical man in stature. I don't mean to be shallow, but I found it impossible to stop staring at him. Without even removing his sage green masquerade mask, he still looked like a movie star.

Perhaps I was delusional. That, or I had too much to drink.

I had been walking over to the bar area away from the ballroom floor when we locked eyes. I averted my gaze as his piercing stare made me feel like I was the prey of a ferocious lion. His aura of confidence was overwhelming and his gaze filled me with a feeling of insignificance. That being said, I had become accustomed to feeling small. Nonetheless, I knew how to navigate my insecurities; I was not going to let his looks intimidate me, in spite of how alluring or magnetic he appeared to be.

But it seemed like there wasn't a way out, that there was no time to decide. He walked right up to me as I was heading to the bar. Many different scenarios played out in my head as my mind attempted to foretell what would happen next. I had become completely entranced by the grandeur of this man, so much so that I had momentarily forgotten I was in an opulent mansion filled with top tech executives. My entire attention was fixed on this one man.

I felt my cheeks flush as I felt his piercing gaze against my own. I couldn't comprehend why he was so interested in me, a mere employee, among the people of greater importance in the IT field. Was I reading too much into his curious glances? I felt my femininity surge at the thought that he was attracted to me in this festive Mardi Gras atmosphere. Everyone around us was adorned in bright masks, adding to the energy, and I wondered if his gaze was one of desire or if he misconstrued me as someone of great power. Of course, I couldn't ignore the possibility that he may have just wanted to know the time.

"I don't mean to offend you, but I'm quite glad you're wearing a mask," he said, nonchalantly. Puzzled, I stood there in humiliation. "Because now I can really focus on just how beautiful your eyes are. Care for a dance?" I was taken aback by the gravelly baritone of his voice. It wasn't every day that a man like him would approach me, and I was certainly not prepared for it. His jawline was so sharp, it was like it had been carved from stone. Though it was unexpected, I found myself enjoying the unpredictability of the situation, and a rush of adrenaline flowed through me.

"I wouldn't mind dancing with you at all," I said. I then added, with a hint of sarcasm, "But please, don't ever use that pick-up line again."

The man let out a hearty chuckle: “I don’t plan on it, now that I’ve met you.” Whoever he was. Hearing his laughter filled me with an unexpected sense of satisfaction. His amusement seemed to break down my defenses, and I felt powerless to him.

Walking me to the dance floor, he said, “You're not going to believe me, but I never use pick-up lines." I rolled my eyes. "Either way, I meant every word. Your eyes are gorgeous."

As I was trying to be in the present moment, I found myself analyzing every word he said and enjoying the lighthearted banter. I felt energized, as if I was solving a crossword puzzle. I was filled with creativity and inspiration. I wanted to keep talking with this attractive stranger, to be in his sphere of influence but still receive the conversation. The word "stimulating" seemed to have lost its definition.

"Thank you, really," I said in all sincerity. "But alas, the dance floor awaits."

When he grabbed my hand and led me to the dance floor, I was speechless. It felt surreal, like a dream that had come to life. As we stepped onto the floor, the room seemed to disappear, leaving just the two of us in the moment. Time seemed to stand still as we swayed to the music, and I wanted the moment to last forever.

I tried to steady my breathing as I felt the softness of his hand on my waist. His touch was resolute yet gentle, like I was holding a winning lottery ticket in my hands. I felt as if I had been transported somewhere else, and I had to try to remember where I had seen those mask-covered eyes before. His boldness was oddly familiar, though I knew for sure we had never met before. Maybe I had seen someone like him in one too many romantic novels I had read. Whatever it was, I couldn't deny that his presence made my heart race.

"You know, I had no interest in dancing with anyone tonight," he said, which I found rather endearing, despite being well aware that he could have easily been blowing smoke up my ass. Nonetheless, those were the exact words I would have written for him had this been a movie script. Again, I felt as though I had been lifted away from the room entirely. I felt my strength waning as he gazed into my eyes. You'd think I would've used some discretion or restraint in how I maintained my defenses. And then I did something that, given who I was, was uncharacteristically outrageous.

I leaned in, drawn to him like a moth to a flame. Our lips met, sending a jolt of electricity through my body. His stubble felt warm and rough against my lips, and his kiss was wet and passionate. It was like a dream come true, and I felt like I was in paradise.

Chapter 3

♥

Randy

Her mouth was sugary, and her lips matched the sweetness. In every way, they exceeded my wildest expectations. Those cute little pillows puckered every time I flicked my lips across hers. That she wanted me as badly as I wanted her completely shocked me. To put it simply, I was immersed in my own private film.

The best part of our conversation was the fact that I got goosebumps afterward. I had complete control over my life, so it was rare for me to experience such an emotional response. As an affluent person, I was used to instant gratification and the drawbacks that come with it. Money gave me enough to buy the world, but it couldn't give me true emotion. As a result, I knew this woman before me was exceptional because of her ability to do so.

After we broke apart from the kiss, I said, "Well then." Yes, it was seen by a few people, I'm sure.

“I don’t care if you don’t care,” she said, beaming at me.

"I'm not sure which corner of the universe you’re from, but I'm glad you're here,” I said, feeling more assured than ever. “I need you—that might sound forward, but I want to take care of you. From the moment I saw you, I've been dreaming of taking you back to my hotel room and exploring all the possibilities between us.”

She locked eyes with me and let out a sweet little giggle. I could tell she was intrigued by my boldness. I felt the connection between us and knew that I was getting close to sealing the deal. No cheesy pick-up lines needed here; her body language and my sixth sense were enough to tell me that she'd be coming back to my place soon.

We made like we were newlyweds as we stepped through the doorway of my hotel room, and as she looked up at me with her delicate features, she pulled me in for a passionate kiss. Our mouths moved in perfect harmony, tongues exploring and hands caressing each other's faces. She felt so small in my arms, yet with each touch, she seemed to grow bolder, her desire for me becoming more evident. I was grateful for my unshaven stubble as it provided her with a pleasing sensation as her lips brushed against it. Never before had I been so aroused by someone so small, yet so powerful in her passion.

I carried her to my bed like a prized possession, my hands caressing her hair. As I set her down, I could sense the electricity between us. She looked up at me with a sly grin, as if she knew what I was about to do. I take great pleasure in being the one in control, and it seemed she was more than happy to be restrained by me. After all, my years of experience as a CEO and owner had taught me the art of dominance. Though my wealth was the result of hard work, I had to admit that a mastery of domination was a welcome bonus.

My eyes were drawn to her as she lay face down on the bed, her demeanor invitingly submissive. A spark of desire lit in her eyes and her expression softened in response. I couldn't help but smile, feeling a warmth of contentment that she was in my hotel room. I wanted to get to know her better and, though we were both wearing masks, I was confident that our connection would only deepen with time.

I carefully undid the dress and admired her tiny, shapely body. Her curves were delectable and her frame was slim and toned. She was wearing nothing but a mask and a bra, the sight of which sent a thrill of anticipation through me. With each passing second, I felt the bond between us grow stronger.

At that moment, neither of us could make much sense of anything. Okay, maybe I should have spoken up for myself. The connection between us was immediate and effortless. They happened at the same time, that much is certain. That prompted me to remove her bra, too. Piece by piece, the cloth made its way down her thighs. My dick got stiffer as more of her slit emerged. To begin, I noticed a stray hair in my peripheral vision. This was followed by the introduction of the lips.

I couldn't believe my eyes when I saw her. A stunning woman wearing a mask and baring her pussy to the crowd. She had an incredible physique—her curves tantalizing me with every step she took. I wanted to strip her down to her titties and taste her delicious skin. I was spellbound, my gaze tracing the lines of her thighs. I could feel the desire coursing through my veins, urging me to take her in my arms and make her mine.

I chose to make the most of my stay in the hotel and do something special. So I decided to treat myself to an unforgettable experience—tasting her. I couldn't resist the temptation and I had to have a lick of her sweet nectar.

My tongue glided against the sweet, salty flavor of her pussy, its moisture filling me with an eagerness to please her. I could feel her body responding to each flick of my tongue; small moans escaped her lips as I increased my speed and aggression. I was pleased to know my work was paying off, and my libido surged with each touch. She was like a harp for me to play, and my dick was growing harder and harder with each movement. As her body welcomed me closer, I could feel myself ready to take her to new heights of pleasure.

My heart raced as I undid my belt, the anticipation coursing through my veins. She watched me with a look of pure delight, her eyes hidden beneath the mask. I felt like I already knew her body intimately, the mystery of her face hidden behind the fabric driving me wild with desire. I carefully inserted my shaft into her and I could feel her joy as I did. Her pleasure was palpable, and it only made me even more aroused. I could feel every inch of her as I thrust, the sensation sending a wave of pleasure throughout my body. I felt as if I was almost there, the sheer intensity of our love-making leading me to the brink. Add all that up and you have a tremendous orgasm. At least, that's what I assumed would happen. However, I hadn't cum yet.

My dick surged in and out of her, each thrust a wave of pleasure that carried me closer to bliss. I could feel her tightness around me, and with each sensation my eyes would flutter shut. Her own expression was a mix of pleasure and awe as I moved in and out of her, and all I could think of was how good it felt. Our movements were like a dance, each thrust sending us deeper and deeper into pleasure until we were lost in the moment.

"Oh my god, yes!" She uttered, her voice trembling with passion and anticipation. I could tell she was embarrassed by the impulsive nature of our encounter, but I could also sense her eagerness to explore this newfound pleasure. I, too, felt the heat of desire coursing through me, knowing that my climax was just a few moments away.

That's precisely what followed. Just in the nick of time, I managed to cum. Two masked strangers just fucked, and I was one of them. A lot of weird stuff has happened in my life. However, this was right up there with the best of them.

Chapter 4

♥

Madison

After he was done, I could feel the intensity of his pleasure through my whole body and I wanted more. I took his hand and pulled him closer, inviting him for a second round. His surprise was evident but I had already given in to the pleasure, and he followed suit. With each thrust, I could feel my toes curl as pleasure rippled through me, intensifying until I reached my climax. His pleasure was so great that I could feel it in my toes as well, and I knew that this round was going to be even more powerful than the first.

At the end of that second session, I felt like a new person entirely. I was no longer confined to my usual facade—I'd found a new kind of freedom that I hadn't known before. I embraced my entire body, from head to toe, as I strutted around with a mask over my face. I felt powerful, strong, and completely in control.

* * *

After we finished showering and changing (yes, with our masks still on all the while), we collapsed next to each other, exhausted yet exhilarated. I had never allowed myself to act in such a way before—taking a risk and engaging in a one-night stand without knowing the identity of the person I was with. I had always been so cautious, taking the time to get to know potential partners before taking the plunge. But that night, I decided to let go of my inhibitions and take a chance on something new. The thrill of the risk and the excitement of the unknown added an electricity to the air that was palpable. The masquerade ball had opened my eyes to a new kind of freedom and to the possibilities of taking risks. No longer would I be confined to the boundaries of my own inhibitions.

He was the one who broke the silence, I didn't have much time to consider everything.

"Well, that just happened, huh?" he said.

"It certainly did," I inched closer, my eyes drawn to his. As I looked into them, the familiarity I'd felt earlier returned. "How often do you have masked sex?"

It was him that laughed this time. "Call me what you'd like, but I'm a sex-mask virgin."

I couldn't help but let out a hearty laugh. It was like a joke-based joust. "In that case, it is my pleasure to have been the one to have taken your sex-mask virginity." I paused, noticing that he was waiting for me to say something. "It's the first time I did it in a mask, too." A sense of relief seemed to have washed over him, as if I had just confirmed that I wasn't any old slut. "I hate to be the one to burst your bubble, but I think it's about time we introduce ourselves."

Suddenly, he faced me. His thick mound of chest hair diverted my attention. A sexy mound of chest hair, might I add. "Honestly, it feels like we should be wearing masks. Our anonymity seems strangely... appropriate," despite the previous series of events being anything but.

"I can't protest," I said, contemplating whether or not to take a plunge and swim in his chest hair. "We may be the only people who have ever had sex while wearing masks. I'm sure there's an exception somewhere, but I can't think of one right now."

With one hand, he rubbed my hair. As he touched it, he felt its texture. In a word, it was sensual. Indeed, it provided some much-needed solace. My heart rate was slowing and I felt calmer. There was something about being in his company that made me feel secure. Again, coming from someone whose face I wouldn't be able to identify had he been without a mask, that was a very strange thing to say. It's equally comforting that someone who I couldn't even see could make me feel that way.

"Then again," he said, causing my heartrate to pick up again, "what a miserable thing it would be to, ya know, cross each other's paths on the street and not be able to recognize one another."

He was right: eventually, we had to see each other's faces. The anticipation was palpable; we were both eager to reveal ourselves. This was meant to be a chance for us to grow closer and build a deeper connection. We had just finished exploring each other's bodies, after all. His member was twitching with pleasure as I watched him reach his climax. He had seen me reach mine. *Hell, he had licked me dry!*

After brushing my hair, he used the same hand to lift my mask. In a way, it was as if he recognized me. But then the flash of insight passed, and he said, "You are beautiful, like, *really*." His awe soon transformed into confusion. "But I'm sure I've seen you somewhere."

A moment passed.

It was now obvious that a look at his face was in order. When he removed his disguise, I instantly knew who he was and I felt an overwhelming sense of regret and rage.

I was only able to mutter one word: "*Skydeck*."

Not too long ago, I had applied for a job at Skydeck, a role in IT. This job would have been a great opportunity for me to further my career as a programmer. As I prepared for the interview, I was filled with a mix of excitement and anxiety. I was determined to do my best and make a good impression.

However, when it came to the interview itself, I was met with an unexpected challenge. The interviewer was unimpressed with my answers and began to verbally berate me. He made me feel stupid and small, and my confidence plummeted. I knew then that my chances of succeeding were slim.

To make matters worse, the interviewer's words had spread and it seemed like everybody in the industry had heard about the incident. I was left feeling helpless and embarrassed. I felt like my professional future had been ruined by one ill-fated interview.

"Randy Maven." Startled, I sat up quickly in the bed, covering my pale breasts with the sheet.

Interesting, it wasn't me knowing his name that startled him; seemingly everyone in this industry knew Randy Maven. Rather, it was the hiding of my breasts that seemed to provoke bewilderment in the man across from me.

"You remember the interview from last year?" I said, summoning what was left of my courage. "The one where you turned my life into a living hell?"

I seethed with rage as I watched the wheels turning in his head. He couldn't remember, and that just fuelled my fury even more. I stormed away from the bed, gathering my clothes as I went. I had no intention of ever seeing this man again—he could go to hell.

Chapter 5

♥

*R*andy

I have never felt so uncomfortable in the presence of a woman before. She seemed so appalled and disgusted by me that she quickly put her clothes on. Her reaction made me feel like an unwelcome intruder, like I was the one inflicting harm.

Recalling the details of the interview, I felt embarrassed. I had been intoxicated that day, and my judgment was severely impaired. I had taken a critical look at her outfit and ridiculed her CV.

I had gone so far as to call the people who had brought her in "idiots." My drinking problem had caused me to feel a sense of arrogance and a false sense of control.

Once I had gone through a recovery program, I was finally able to find a place in society again. I had not consumed any alcohol for over a year and since stopped counting the days. Although I was proud of my progress, I was also aware of the danger of letting go. It was like gripping a massive gold nugget, and if I let go, it would be gone forever.

I was determined to move forward and make a life for myself. I had to focus on the present and the future, instead of dwelling on the past. I was determined to be sober and build a life for myself that didn't involve alcohol. I was also aware that sobriety was a journey and not a destination.

"Hey, come on now! Let me explain!

She scoffed as she pulled her bra over her head. "Let you explain? Are you kidding me? You humiliated me in front of a room full of people simply because I didn't look the way you wanted me to? Because my resume didn't have six internships? I will never forget the embarrassment, disrespect, and discouragement you inflicted on me. But I won't let it stop me from succeeding—and showing you that I'm more than capable of success despite your belittling!" And then, an admission: "I have news for you: I have done more than okay for myself! I'm working in marketing now, at a rival company—Umbrella Enterprises! And I'm sure you've heard of them!"

My company had an adversary called Umbrella, which was an undeniable fact. Although it was annoying to discover that the girl I had just had sex with wearing a mask worked for my competitor and held a grudge against me, they were still a long way from achieving the same level of success as us.

“Please, Madison,” I said. She was surprised and appalled that I recalled her name. “Can I just explain myself, please?”

“There's absolutely nothing to explain. You ruined my life and I regret ever having sex with you,” she said, her voice raising into a crescendo. “Do you understand me, *Randall*? Take a look at my vagina, because you're never going to see it again.” She motioned toward her groin, but I averted my eyes. “Remember what you just did, because it will never happen again. You will never see me again—not ever! I'm so furious with you and I will never forgive you for what you did.”

The woman's scathing remarks were enough to make me realize that any further interactions with her were off the table. As soon as I realized what I had done, I was overcome with a deep sense of despondency and guilt. The thought of the night

I got drunk with that guy came flooding back and suddenly, all the effort I had put into improving myself seemed to be for nothing.

"OK, I won't say another word.

I watched sadly as she pulled her thong up her legs, my last chance of seeing her beautiful body gone. I was going to miss her and the time we spent together. But I had to accept that she wasn't interested in me and try to move on. As she put on the rest of her clothes, I knew that I had to find a way to get over her.

The slamming of the door shook the entire room. Door slammed, a motivation grew inside me like no other. I couldn't believe it; she had just left me. I was determined to get her back, no matter the cost. I had to find a way to make her understand that I was not the person she saw in the interview. My addiction had caused that situation and I had put it behind me.

I rose from my bed and paced around the room, my mind spinning with possibilities. I had been successful in the business world and had grown my company to one of the biggest in the world. I had knowledge, resources and creativity—surely there must be a way to get her back. I just had to be inventive and find the answer.

I finally had an aha moment — I had to acquire her business. Despite the fact that it sounded awful, I knew it was the only way to reconnect with her and show her I had matured. I wouldn't put her job in danger, but rather I wanted to buy her company so I could spend more time with her and get to know her better. It was a win-win situation — I could reconnect with her and she wouldn't have to worry about her job. And it was a decision I was happy to make.

A decision which would allow me to see the lady in the red dress once more.

Chapter 6

♥

Madison

The Twitter headline was unreal. I couldn't take my eyes off it; hell, I even pinched myself!

TRENDING: Randy Maven buys Umbrella**.**

I felt so insignificant at that moment. It was like a scene from a Disney movie, where the villain was using his power in an unrealistic way to try and ruin my life because I had rejected him. Was he trying to flex? Was it some sort of twisted power play? I didn't care. The upside was that I was the protagonist in this story, and the protagonist always comes out on top in the end. Who was kidding themselves here? Certainly not me.

My palms grew sweaty and my heart raced as I anticipated Randy walking in and flipping my desk. My mind ran wild with irrational thoughts. But I knew one thought was certain: he bought the company because of me. That was power. *No, it was spite.*

The big question was whether he had done it maliciously. In the bedroom, his demeanor seemed genuine, and he appeared sincere. Alternatively, he may have been embarrassed. It was difficult to assess the situation accurately since he was behaving in the presence of a naked woman. He had purchased the company for reasons that were not clear to me, reasons that would take months to become apparent.

"Good morning, Madison," said a gravelly voice from behind me. "What a beautiful morning, isn't it?"

I hated to admit it, but I was still attracted to him. Even though he had ruined my life at one point, I couldn't deny the fact that he was still incredibly sexy. It was a constant internal struggle for me—my feelings for him were so strong, but I knew I had to keep them in check. As 9:30 am rolled around and my coffee buzz wore off, I realized that I was too exhausted to start the mental battle of my conflicting emotions. So, I chose to keep my back to him and my feelings to myself. It was for the best.

"Would you mind turning around?" he persisted.

I felt completely taken aback when he asked me this. It felt like he was breaking down the boundaries that I had worked so hard to build up.

It was like having an unwelcome guest enter my life.

"I understand that you are my boss and the owner of this place," I said, "but frankly, I don't think turning around in this chair is part of my job description. I need to focus on my work. So, if you'd please—"

"You're really going to make me fight for this, huh?"

Buying this company was one of the worst decisions you ever made in your career, if I'm being completely honest. It was completely unnecessary and, with all due respect *boss*, nothing you say or do is going to make me take notice, no matter how professional you try to be."

He paused.

"Professional?" he said. "The only way you'd dare speak to me is if it concerns business matters?"

"You heard me."

"Speaking of business, I've actually been looking for a new assistant." I froze. "What, you don't like that? OK, 'secretary' it is, then." I bit my lip in utter fury. "Tough crowd. Anyways, I look forward to talking with you; professional, of course. I'll double your salary too. Meet me in my office tomorrow morning." Before he strutted off, he added, "Oh, and feel free to wear a mask."

I swallowed, trying to stay composed. I heard his footsteps as he walked out of the room, but I refused to turn around and look. My hands were shaking and my heart was pounding. Nothing felt real. I pinched myself again, hoping to wake up from this nightmare. I couldn't understand how I had ended up being hired as an assistant for the man I revile.

Then again, that may be a bit harsh. I may have not known exactly who he was when we had sex, but I must have seen something in him that

I liked. In truth, we were enjoying each other's company before I found out his identity.

I was nervous, my head spinning with a thousand thoughts. Quitting was certainly an option, but my job at one of the world's best companies was too good to pass up. I was trapped, but I knew I had to adapt and make the best of the situation.

Or die trying.

Chapter 7

♥

Randy

As I drove into work, I felt an immense hatred for myself that radiated through my body. I had achieved so much in life, yet I still felt this way. I knew that even the most successful people had moments of self-loathing, and I was no exception. The reason for my anguish was the fact that I was making a woman's life miserable. I had feelings for her, but instead of expressing them, I resorted to tormenting her. My own actions were causing me a great deal of shame and sadness.

She was going to start as my assistant and I had to make sure I was ready to present myself in the best possible light. I was used to being a bit of a charmer and had a reputation as a confident, charismatic guy—but I knew that she was no pushover and I wasn't sure how to handle the situation. I had to find a way to bridge the gap between the person she thought I was, and the person I wanted to be.

She was clearly attracted to me, having experienced the physical chemistry between us, but I was still concerned about how to interact with her. I wished I could go to some sort of boot camp to learn how to deal with emotions in a more productive way. But I had no choice—if I wanted to be with her, I had to play the game. I was confident I could find a way to make her see me differently and I was determined to prove myself.

When I got to the office, I placed my coffee down on the desk and did a little stretching to get myself ready for what was about to come. I had twenty minutes until Madison's arrival and I had no idea what to expect. Would she come in with a scowl on her face or a sarcastic smile? I had no way of predicting what her reaction would be, and that made it hard to prepare. Even in something like war, you had some idea of what to expect; not with love.

I sat in my office, sipping my coffee and doing anything I could to pass the time. I was trying to distract myself from the impending arrival of her, the one I was waiting for. I didn't want to be sitting there, anxious and overthinking when she arrived. I wanted things to feel natural and comfortable. So I busied myself with work, checking my spreadsheets, taking calls and responding to emails, anything to keep my mind off her.

I glanced at the clock, thirty minutes past when my new assistant was set to arrive, and sighed in frustration. Just as I was about to take a deep breath and try to figure out what had happened, Harry from human resources popped his head in the doorway. "Hey Randy, your new assistant called out for the day," he said, uncaring.

"But it's her first day," I said as though he actually cared. Harry couldn't have cared less about her being just an employee, but I needed to vent a little bit. I just wanted someone to give me an ear and make me feel less insane.

Harry shrugged and said, "I don't know what to tell you. I guess you'll just have to fire her." He walked away.

I stared at the empty chair across from me, my mind racing with unanswered questions. My plan had been thwarted, and I was at a loss as to how to proceed. My heart was heavy, and I was filled with a mix of emotions I couldn't quite identify.

Was she really not coming in the next day? Would she quit entirely? I felt a desperate urge to have some sort of resolution, but I was unsure of how to go about it. The chair seemed to mock me, reminding me of my failed mission, and I felt a deep sense of frustration and sadness.

I got up from my desk and stretched, feeling the ache of a plan gone wrong. I had done all I could think of, but I would have to wait until the morning to find out if it was enough.

I always thought it was really cool that we had a little cafe in the building and didn't have to leave to get coffee. At first it was a fun treat, but after a while it became a source of frustration for me. After all, it was one of the main accomplishments I had to show for my time as CEO. So, every time I went to get a coffee, I was reminded of the fact that I hadn't achieved more. Suddenly, I had been transformed into this powerful CEO who seemed to have no regard for the consequences of his actions. This new persona had caused suffering while in the throes of addiction.

For me, the cafe was a reminder that no matter how much money or power you had in the world, happiness can't be bought. Nor can forgiveness. And certainly not love. Ironically, even if I could buy Madison's heart, I wouldn't want to. I want her to want me for who I am.

That day was a setback. But in the corporate world, we see setbacks as an opportunity for growth, and I certainly had no intentions of giving up.

Chapter 8

Madison

I walked up to my desk and fixed my gaze on Randy, arms crossed. His surprise was evident on his face, downright comical.

"I thought you were quitting," he spat out.

"Why? Because I called out yesterday? I needed a day to regroup," she said. "Let me rephrase: I needed a day to be away from you."

"Ouch."

I tried to keep my arms crossed, but his gaze traveled to my chest, causing a spark of desire to stir in my nether regions. I quickly forced myself to remember why I was angry with him and tried to maintain my anger, but I had to admit that a small part of me was glad I had chosen to come to work that day.

"You came in for a reason. Sure, you were getting paid pretty well. But, Madison, I handed you a check with this month's salary the day I bought Umbrella," he said. "You could have easily found another job. I mean, with the *resume* you have—" I felt the embers of my soul light on fire. "What I'm saying is, there's no real reason for you to be working here as my assistant, which, in turn, leads me to believe you don't hate me as much as I originally assumed. Tell me: am I wrong?"

I sighed, needing a moment to think of an appropriate response. "I believe everyone deserves a second chance, but I don't think that applies in this instance. I don't want to stay here, in this office, with you. You caused irreparable damage to my life and buying this company just to be close to me is a flex. It's foolish and unnecessary," she said. "Plus, I don't have the time to search for another job."

"You can think what you want about that man I used to be, but that's not who I am today," he said, with what appeared to be a glimmer of sincerity. "I admit that, in my drunkenness, I made a mistake and it cost me. But I'm here now, and I've spent a fortune to have the chance to talk to you. Frankly, that's the only reason I did all this. Think what you want, but I'm here now, and I'm ready to make a change."

I got up from my desk and locked the door, then strode over to his desk. I spun him around to face me and kissed him without any hesitation; my tongue slipping into his mouth without a second thought. His tongue met mine in a passionate dance. His body radiates warmth and the scent of cinnamon and some other spicy cologne filled my nose. It was like the day we first met... well, more accurately: the day we first met, in masks.

I pulled away, and he gave me a questioning glance. "What was that about?"

"I wanted to see if I still felt anything after knowing you ruined my life." I corrected myself: "I wanted to see if I still felt anything after knowing the man behind the mask."

"And did you?"

I kissed him again.

That was my answer.

I couldn't control my desire. My hands slid across his hard chest, exploring every contour and ripple. His arousal was evident as he grabbed my ass cheeks and pulled me close, making me gasp with pleasure. I wanted him so badly that I climbed onto his lap. His rock-hard erection pressed against my stomach, both of us unable to contain our passions. I unbuttoned his shirt, revealing the soft yet coarse hair on his chest. I ran my fingers through it, letting it prickle my skin with pleasure. His chest hair was like a brush of fire, igniting my desire and making me ache with need.

I couldn't keep my hands off him. His body was like an electric current, and I felt it surging through me. I leaned in to kiss his neck, my lips leaving a trail of fire as I moved. His hands moved around me, pulling me in closer. We weren't in an office anymore; we were in the sky. I could feel the euphoria radiating through my body as we kissed. Every move I made seemed to increase the intensity of the pleasure I felt, and I wanted him more and more. I wanted to explore every inch of his body, to feel the warmth of his skin against mine. My desire for him was like a wildfire, and I wanted to fulfill it in every way possible.

He grabbed both my ass cheeks firmly and massaged them with all his fingers. I felt myself melting beneath his touch, my anger and frustration forgotten as his hands explored my curves. With a sudden tug, he yanked my skirt down, exposing my bare ass cheeks to the chilly air of the room. I gasped in surprise as the fabric left my skin, my ass cheeks bouncing a little with the sudden movement. His hands moved to the thong, and with a swift tug, pulled it down as well, leaving me completely exposed and vulnerable to his gaze.

He said something that caught me off guard at first: "*Take a look at my vagina,*" he quoted me word-for-word, *“because you're never going to see it again.*” I rolled my eyes and laughed. God, he was sexy.

He didn't know that I was drenched between my legs, desperately awaiting his touch. I wanted his tongue to explore me, to make me writhe in pleasure.

But I had to put my grudge against him aside and focus on the moment. I was ready to see what would happen next.

Chapter 9

♥

Randy

I had her on my desk. All the papers have been thrown on the floor. I even knocked my laptop over. Her legs were spread wide open, and I could see the glistening of her pussy lips. I was mesmerized by the sight of her shaved pussy, the fresh smell of her radiating off of her. I was so overwhelmed by the beauty of her that I was almost unable to contain myself.

I started to lick her pussy with a deliberate speed, determined to please her and show her that I cared. I took my time, and let my tongue dance around her. I took note of her reactions, and adjusted my movements accordingly. I was pushing the boundaries, pushing further and further into her, making her moan louder and louder, and I could feel her body quivering with pleasure.

The sensations I was feeling were too much to contain, and I had to let out a moan of my own. I kept my eyes on her, taking in her beauty, and watching her facial expressions as I licked her. Her eyes were auburn, and were captivating. They were like portals, leading to a different universe. I was entranced, and unable to look away.

The feeling of her wetness was intoxicating, and her moans were enough to drive me wild. I kept going, pushing my tongue further and further, and I could feel her body trembling with pleasure. Eventually, she pulled my head away from her pussy, and looked me in the eyes.

I was completely spent, and my body was trembling with exhaustion. I had shown her that I cared, and I could tell she was satisfied. We had created a bond through our sexual activities, and I could feel that connection. It was an incredible experience, and one that I will never forget.

"I want you to fuck me," she admitted, "No, I need you to."

I stepped towards her and unzipped my pants, my rock hard cock begging for release. She watched with wide eyes as I pulled my pants and boxers down, exposing it to her. I could feel the desire radiating from her and it only intensified my own.

I took her in my arms and pressed her against me, my hard cock entering her wet depths with ease. She felt amazing, so tight and slippery at the same time. I started to thrust in and out, harder and faster with each movement.

The best part was I could finally see her face, her eyes closed and her expression full of pleasure. I could feel the sensations building up inside her, the pleasure and passion growing with every thrust. I wanted to make her cum, I wanted to feel that satisfaction that comes with giving someone else pleasure.

I kept going, and she kept getting closer and closer to the edge with every movement. Her breasts bounced with each thrust, her bra not enough to prevent the movement. I watched with lust as her body stiffened, her orgasmic cries filling the room. I felt my own orgasm coming and I yanked myself out of her, spilling my cum on the floor.

She kept cumming, her body shaking with pleasure. When it was over we both looked at each other in awe, amazed at what had just occurred. Neither of us had ever had sex in the office before, especially not our own.

We both laughed, the tension broken, and I pulled her onto my lap. We shared a few more laughs before getting up and getting dressed. We both knew we'd never forget what had just happened. We'd just experienced something we'd both remember forever.

"I guess you christened this office, huh?" she said

"There's no better way to christen an office than with a pussy like yours," I retorted, which caused her to let out a hearty laugh that seemed to echo through the room.

"All right, let's put our clothes on before the scandal gets out."

We both quickly got dressed and awkwardly stood behind our desks, pretending nothing had happened. We both felt relieved when she opened the door and saw that no one was around. However, the reality of the situation settled in, and I was left feeling a mix of emotions.

"Shit," I uttered. “The camera.”

Madison's face flushed with embarrassment as her gaze settled on the menacingly glossy black security camera in the corner of the room.

"Don't worry, I'll handle it."

I dialed the security room number on my office phone, listening to the ringtones echoing through the receiver. "Hey, it's Randy. I need everyone out of that office, *now*."

I rose from my chair and turned to face Madison, reassuring her with a confident tone. "I have security clearance for that room," I said, "so you can rest assured that the tape won't be leaked and that everything will be erased."

"What about the people who are looking at the camera right now?"

"I'm the CEO, so the camera only kicks in when I hit the panic button. It records, but it's not a live feed," I reassured her. She seemed to comprehend what I said, but appeared doubtful.

"Madison. I wouldn't let anything get out like that. Relax"

I shut the door, then leaned in and kissed her.

"I believe you," she said. "Just *promise* me that tape will never get out."

"I won't, baby. I promise."

I intended to keep that promise.

Chapter 10

♥

Madison

The morning after our passionate night together, I was filled with a mix of emotions while I sat at my desk, eagerly awaiting his arrival. Despite my lingering hesitation, I had allowed myself to let my walls down. Instead of the solid, impenetrable fortress I had built to protect myself, my walls had become a pile of bricks, providing only a slight buffer between us. Although I wasn't sure if it was wise to be so trusting, I couldn't deny the change I felt inside. Things felt different.

Just being at work, I was overwhelmed with a feeling of euphoria. My heart raced and my hands grew clammy as I watched my boss enter the office. I felt a strong pull to be closer to him, to engage in conversation and to bask in his presence. The thought of being around him gave me a thrill, like anything could happen between us, separated only by two desks. I felt a giddy joy that was hard to describe, unable to contain the excitement that consumed me.

The fear that ate away at me was the knowledge that it had all been caught on camera. But I had to trust Randy when he said that he had taken care of it. As a woman who cherished her own body and saw it every single day, the thought of that intimate moment being spread outside of that room would be catastrophic. It would be like Randy had ruined my life twice. I tried not to dwell on that thought, but it was hard to not be pessimistic in such a situation.

Randy's sudden interruption jarred me from my daydreaming, as he peered into the office with a mischievous glint in his eye. "Let's play hooky today," he proposed. "No one has to know—just you and me. A date of sorts. We'll say that you're accompanying me to a business meeting. How does that sound?"

The tenderness of the man's sentiment made my heart race and my cheeks flush. It was only nine-thirty in the morning, but his spontaneous gesture filled me with warmth and admiration. His willingness to follow through with his passionate promise left me in awe, and I felt my lips curl into a smile as I replied, "I would love that."

"Well then, leave your desk and follow me."

As I followed closely behind Randy, my CEO, I couldn't help but take note of the astonished stares that were thrown our way. After all, it wasn't every day that the head of the company was trailed by his assistant as we walked through the office halls like a celebrity and their bodyguard. I was aware of the envy that was radiating from the cubicles, but I couldn't bring myself to care too much. I had earned my spot in the company and I was determined to make the most of it. The moment we stepped into the elevator, I was thrown headfirst into a cloud of spicy cologne. I closed my eyes and inhaled the aroma for a few seconds before I was brought back to the present. I knew it was going to be a day to remember.

"Ever think you'd be skipping work to go on a date with the CEO?" He asked me after pressing the down button.

Once the door was closed I said, "No, for two reasons. One, because 'the CEO' as of a few days ago was a 60-year-old woman named Paula. Two, because I had no intentions on talking to you before— well, you know," she blushed. "When it comes to you, Randy, there's a lot I didn't expect to happen, but I'm glad that they all did. If I ever had a comfort zone, that thing was blown to bits a *long* time ago."

I noticed his eyes start to drift down to my lips as he moved closer to me. A wave of anticipation and excitement rushed through me and I felt my heart beat pick up. But then, he abruptly stopped and his gaze shifted to the elevator camera in the corner. I felt a pang of disappointment, but I was also relieved. He spoke, his voice soft and gentle. "I know you saw what I just did. I'm trying to be respectful and not ruin your reputation by being with me. Just don't ever take it that I don't want to be seen with you or something. Because that's not the case. I just don't want you getting treated differently, you know what I mean?" I nodded, feeling my cheeks flush. I appreciated his consideration and I knew that he was trying to do the right thing.

I stood there, silently, my eyes shut tight as I searched for the perfect words to express my gratitude. After a few moments of thought, I opened my eyes and looked into his. "You know, this is the kind of thing that really makes me trust you. It's one of the most thoughtful things anyone has done for me and it really shows how much you care."

He chuckled, a deep and throaty sound that made my heart flutter. I couldn't understand why he was amused, until he said, "If that's the nicest thing anyone's done for you, you've lived an awfully terrible life. " His words were kind, but there was an edge of sadness beneath them. His expression softened, and I could see the genuine concern in his eyes.

Chapter 11

♥

Randy

Madison's reaction to being in a limousine for the first time was unforgettable. Her eyes had grown wide, and she nervously glanced around the car, almost as if she was trying to pretend she was used to this kind of luxury. Her cheeks were flushed and her hands were shaking, yet her excitement was obvious. It was like a child in a candy store—overwhelmed, yet determined to take it all in.

My own wealth and opulence seemed insignificant in comparison to the moment. Even my immense bank account and sprawling mansion couldn't replace the pure bliss radiating from Madison's face. Money couldn't buy the joy of experiencing something for the first time, and I was more than happy to be able to witness it. It was a moment of innocence, unadulterated by the influence of wealth and power.

"I take it you've never been in a limousine before," which caused her cheeks to immediately turn a bright shade of pink. I couldn't help but chuckle at the sight, but I quickly tried to cover it up with a polite smile.

"How could you tell?"

"You have a tell," I said. "Your cheeks blush when you're nervous. It's quite cute, actually."

Her cheeks were still flushed a deep shade of red as she questioned, "Oh, is that so? What else do you notice about me that I don't notice myself?"

"When you get quiet, I can tell that you're taking everything in," I said. "You're good at that, even though you didn't recognize me under the mask. You bite your lip when you're thinking, and you look at the ground when you're bashful. And when you get turned on, you get really shy."

"Alright, I think that's enough. We're in a limo with a driver up front, and I don't want him hearing all this. But I'm really flattered that you picked up so much about me. You're certainly different from the guy who laughed at me during my first interview with the other company."

I nodded, feeling like it was the perfect time to clear the air. "I know I gave you a brief about what happened, but I owe you more than that. Back then, I had a really bad drinking problem. I had hit the peak of success but I wasn't happy, and so I started drinking in the morning, at work, when I came home. I felt invincible, getting away with it, and you caught the tail end of that. It took an intervention at work and rehab for me to get my act together, and I'm so grateful that I did. I wouldn't risk it for the world now that I have you. I'm so sorry for what I did in that interview. You didn't deserve it, and neither did anyone else. I was a dick. The only good thing that came from it was me helping the mayor get clean, too, before he won office."

She looked at me with sympathetic eyes, perhaps even with a hint of pity. I knew I deserved it; my story was a pathetic one, but I was glad I had told her. That much was out in the open now.

"I know this may sound strange, but I don't resent you for what happened," she said. "It still stings when I think of it, a terrible memory I wish I didn't have to associate with you. But at the same time, I can separate those two men: him and the one currently sitting across from me. Drunk Randy is not the Randy I know. We're still new to each other, still learning about one another. I always want to trust you, but if I ever sense the old Randy coming back, then I won't be here any longer."

I actually kind of enjoyed her stern warning. Usually, I wasn't someone that enjoyed being told what to do or following rules. But she was so alluring when she said what she said that I wanted to obey her. I knew I had to be better, I had to be the man she needed me to be. I didn't want Drunk Randy to come back, I despised that version of myself. No amount of money could ever measure up to the beauty and innocence that Madison radiated.

"Madison, I give you my word that I won't betray or hurt you. I know that it's hard to believe, but I hope I've given you enough reasons to trust me by now. I understand the importance of our relationship and I value it more than any stock in my portfolio. I wouldn't be taking you in this limo if I didn't care about you. I wouldn't have bought

Umbrella Enterprises if I didn’t care about you. Hell, I certainly wouldn’t have opened up about my dark past if I didn’t care about you."

She smiled. "I care about you too, Randy," she said. "You can trust that."

I never expected her words to be so comforting, but they were. I wanted to cling to her for as long as I could. Even so, I couldn't shake the feeling that things would not be as straightforward as I had hoped. I was used to difficulties in life, but I desperately wanted to be wrong this time.

Would the other shoe drop? I really hope not. But something told me that everything with Madison was just too damn good to be true.

Chapter 12

♥

Madison

Sitting in the limousine, I felt a strange combination of awe and disbelief. Everything seemed surreal, as if I was living out a dream I had never dared to imagine. It was a far cry from the life I had always thought I would have, yet I felt like I had arrived at something. I didn't know what it was, but I think everyone has a vision of themselves riding in a luxurious car with a wealthy person. That's what I was doing.

The limo came to a stop and I was surprised to see a helicopter waiting for us in the middle of an open field. I hadn't expected that we had traveled so far from our starting point. Despite my surprise, I trusted Randy and stepped out of the vehicle.

"I hope you're not afraid of flying."

I was terrified. Randy had a way of comforting you without even trying. I had this weird notion in my head that if the helicopter were to go down, he could somehow save me. "Of course I'm getting on this helicopter, but where are you taking me? I've heard stories about rich people doing terrible things to very pretty women."

He laughed and extended his hand to help me into the helicopter. His blue eyes sparkled with amusement as he said, "Only thing that I would do to you, I've already done it to you. Twice. One time in a mask," he said, shortly thereafter adding,

"I mean, we can always do it in the mask again. That's completely up to you."

I laughed as we adjusted our seatbelts and prepared for takeoff. The engine roared as the blades of the helicopter began to spin, lifting us up into the sky. I felt a rush of excitement as I watched the ground below us grow smaller and smaller until it was just a tiny speck in the distance. I couldn't help but think about what my life had become; one moment I was getting coffee and the next I was soaring through the clouds on a journey with a man who I fucked in a mask. I knew I needed to stop reflecting and just start living, and this seemed like the perfect opportunity to do that!

The terrain beneath us was awe-inspiring, with the small towns, mountains, and rivers below shrinking to miniature size. I had been on planes before, but the helicopter ride seemed to lend a special kind of magic to the experience. This added to the majesty that Randy exuded: a natural majestic presence that made it impossible not to look up to him.

As we touched down on the small island, my eyes widened in awe—and a tad bit of unease. It was as if I had stepped into a scene from a fairy tale. Everywhere I looked, there were palm trees adorned with bright, colorful masquerade masks, giving the island a cheerful atmosphere. I felt a rush of excitement as I admired the colorful decorations, and I couldn't help but feel like I was in a magical land.

"This is where I got the idea to throw the masquerade ball. They call this place Masquerade Island. I purchased it awhile back as a vacation spot close to the job. I thought it'd be particularly fitting to take you here."

I let out a relieved chuckle. "Geez, these masks really gave me a fright! For a second there,

I thought I'd stumbled into my own horror movie."

He pulled me in close and gave me a tender kiss on my forehead. It had been a long time since I had experienced a forehead kiss and it made my heart flutter. I wanted to stay in his arms forever, and I knew that if I played my cards right, I could make that wish come true.

We were lying in bed together in his vacation home, the air around us thick with anticipation. I could feel the heat radiating from his body and the electricity that seemed to be crackling between us like sparks from a campfire. We were fully clothed, but I could feel something was about to happen. It was like I could sense the fire smoldering beneath the surface, just waiting for the perfect moment to ignite.

"This is really nice. Especially given the fact that I thought I was going to be sitting behind a desk for the entire day," I told him while looking into his eyes on the bed. As always, just being in his presence made the rest of the world completely melt away. The worst thing about being on a private island was the fact that I never wanted to leave it.

"I'm really pleased that you're enjoying the time we're spending together. I wanted to make up for what I did and show you how much I care. I'm always trying to think of ways to wow you."

I giggled. "You've already wowed me, Randy. Believe me. You don't have to keep trying." I paused. "But I do have one request."

"What's that?"

"Take my clothes off and fuck me."

Randy's face lit up with a mischievous smile, and my heart raced with anticipation. I could tell something exciting was coming, and I couldn't help but enjoy the thrill of the unknown.

His eyes glinted with a playfulness that was so characteristic of him, and I knew that this moment was going to be special, with both of us together.

Chapter 13

♥

Randy

My head was on the pillow and Madison's head was positioned between my legs. She greedily sucked on my manhood, her cheeks hollowed out as if she was trying to inhale it. I could tell she was relishing the sensation, as her lips were drawn tightly around me and her eyes were shut tight in concentration. Every movement of her lips and tongue sent waves of pleasure radiating through me.

The girl moved her head up and down my shaft with fervor. Every few seconds, she would take my dick out of her mouth and give it a few delicate licks before continuing her passionate ministrations. Her lips were soft as they grazed up and down the length of me, and her gentle kisses sent waves of pleasure through my body. Those small kisses, more than anything else, made me feel wanted and desired. With her presence and passion, I could feel my arousal grow and I soon could no longer hold back.

She held the base of my cock with one hand and began to suck. Her soft lips felt incredible on my sensitive skin, sending waves of pleasure through my body. With each gentle suck and lick, I felt myself getting closer and closer to the edge of ecstasy. I was right on the brink of cumming when I had to force myself to lift her head away, leaving me with a sweet, lingering sensation as I struggled to regain my composure.

"No. I want you to finish."

"But I want to fuck you," I told her.

"I want to taste you," she insisted.

My heart was pounding as her lips encircled my throbbing member. Her hot breath caressed my skin, sending shivers of pleasure through my body. I could feel my pulse racing as she worked her magic, her tongue swirling around it. I felt like I was in some kind of trance, unable to move or even think.

I could feel the sensations building up in me as her lips closed around my member and she began to suck. I felt my orgasm building up and I gasped as my pleasure crested and spilled out of me.

The feeling was unlike anything I had ever experienced before, and before I knew it my body was tensing up and I was ejaculating right into her mouth. I watched her swallow, our eyes locked in a deep, intimate moment, and I was overwhelmed with a feeling of closeness I had never felt with a woman before. All I could do was surrender myself to the pleasure she was giving me.

My gaze drifted down to her chest, taking in the sight of her bare breasts. Her creamy skin was smooth and flawless, her nipples perky and perfectly round. I felt my heart flutter as I looked at her, a wave of desire washing over me. She seemed to be just as affected by my presence, her breath coming in short gasps as she stared back at me. I allowed myself a small smile of satisfaction, basking in the knowledge that I could turn her on without any effort.

"Why wouldn't I? You just brought me to a private island. You changed my life in many ways. It's the least I can do."

I laughed. "You know I would try to repay you somehow for just doing that but there's nothing that equates to swallowing my, you know, stuff."

There was a thoughtful pause on her end.
I couldn't help but wonder what was going

through her mind. She had that introspective look on her face.

"What's the matter?" I asked her.

She gave a slight shrug, her shoulders barely lifting before dropping back down. Her eyes averted as she looked away. It was clear she didn't want to talk about whatever was on her mind, and I couldn't help but wonder what it was. I felt a wave of embarrassment wash over me, my mind running through every possible scenario. Had I done something wrong? Was there something wrong with my ejaculate? I felt my cheeks flush as the thought crossed my mind.

"Come on Madison. We've come all this way. You can tell me anything. I promise," I reassured her.

She gave me her eyes once more and said, "I guess I'm at the point where I'm afraid you're gonna hurt me." *Whew—so my cum's fine, then!* "You're a billionaire. You could have everything that you want. I'm afraid that you're going to realize that this is crazy for you. Why aren't you with some Victoria's Secret model?."

It was heartbreaking to hear her words, like she had no faith in herself. I didn't even know how to begin helping her to feel worthy. I could relate to her in a way, since I too often felt unworthy and inadequate. How could I possibly give her the confidence she lacked?

"Madison, I'm not a wordsmith. I never have been. Business is my strong suit; romance, not so much. But you, you've changed my life—for the better. You've humbled me and made me appreciate the little things in life. So all I can say is, the impact you've had on me is incredible. I've never brought anyone to this private island before, so that should tell you how special you are to me. You need to recognize your own worth and the effect you've had on me. You're different, and I want you to know that your value is immeasurable."

It felt like I had accomplished something when I saw the look of assurance on her face. Our little moment was, however, abruptly broken when my phone started buzzing like crazy. Text after text kept coming in.

"I guess I should handle this," I said.

My hands shook as I stared at my phone in shock and horror. There, in front of me, were screenshots of Madison and me having sex in the office. I could see the warnings from my staff that someone had posted the footage online. It was clear that the security office had been breached and the images had been leaked. But the worst part was that Madison was exposed for the world to see. I had to act quickly to contain the damage and protect her reputation. The urgency of the situation weighed heavily on my shoulders as I scrambled to find a way to take the images down and erase the evidence of what had happened.

My heart raced as I felt the color drain from my face. I was sure there was no way to hide the truth from Madison—the truth that I had just discovered. If I was to remain the honest man she trusted, I had to be honest with her about this.

When I glanced at her, I immediately felt a pang of guilt. There she was, standing in this secluded island paradise that I had taken her to, and I couldn't bring myself to spoil the moment with the bad news I was about to give her.

I was about to really mess up.

Chapter 14

Madison

As soon as Randy got that text, it was time to go. The change on the island was obvious, but I refused to be the type of woman to demand what was going on. I knew I had to respect his privacy.

On the ride back to the office, I tried to push away my curiosity and focus on trusting Randy. I was better than being insecure.

Though I wanted to know what was going on, I had to do it in a civil manner. I asked him a few questions about his phone—not to pry, but to show that I care. He explained that he was just dealing with some work matters, and I appreciated that he was honest with me.

He didn't have to be, but I was glad that he trusted me enough to share. That was the most important thing—the trust between us. I knew that no matter what happened on the island, our relationship would remain strong.

"Hey, can I ask you a question without it coming off weird?" I asked Randy.

"Yeah, of course." He didn't look at me when he spoke. For whatever reason, that felt like another red flag.

"Did something happen? Because we kind of left that island pretty abruptly. I know you have a busy life but, I don't know, your entire mood has shifted."

"No, I'm good. I guess I just had a realization that we had to go home, you know. We can't live on an island forever," he nervously chuckled. "I forgot I had some business to attend to and um—of course I don't regret going to the island, but I also realized that I fell behind on my work. Work hard, play hard, you know?"

Okay. There was another red flag. I was feeling uneasy. His words had taken a sharp turn, and it was a complete 360 from the way he had been with me until then. I was used to being open with him, but this was different. Something was off and I felt a little worried. Maybe I was just being too sensitive, but I needed to take a step back and realize that not everything was about me. I couldn't keep being so insecure. I had to stay strong for my mental health. I wanted to show him that I trusted him, and I did. I just had to remain calm and not let my emotions get the best of me.

The ride felt different without our usual chatter. We usually talked and joked, but this time there was only the sound of the road. I felt anxious and unsure, but he remained silent and still. The silence was almost oppressive, and I could feel the tension in the air. I was relieved when we finally reached our destination.

Then, when we left the limo, things were still a bit awkward. We walked back inside the building to the office without saying a word to each other. Even in the elevator, the tension was palpable. It wasn't until we reached the office that I knew I had to clear the air once more.

"Randy, I'm not going crazy. You're a totally different person from that island. What the hell's going on? You're freaking me out a little bit."

"Madison," he snapped. I was taken back by the fact that he snapped. I had never seen him frustrated. Not once. I had seen him act like a dick when he was drunk. But I never saw Randy angry. I definitely didn't like it. "I'm sorry. I didn't mean to snap at you. But when I say nothing is wrong, nothing is wrong. Okay? I can't make that anymore clear."

I sat down at my desk, feeling a sense of worry in my stomach. He hadn't even looked at me when I attempted to talk to him. I wanted to keep prying, but I decided to let it go instead. I was so worried that I was going to discover a different side of him, one that I didn't know. All I wanted was to feel like I really knew him, but it was impossible now.

I had one problem though. It was the fact that it was hard not to snap at him for how he snapped at me. Luckily he said, "I'm sorry, all right? Really. I just— if there was something I had to say to you, I would say it... I promise."

Relief washed over me, but my suspicions lingered. I knew there was more to the story than he was letting on. I was no fool; I could tell when someone was keeping secrets. But I had no way to uncover his thoughts. I was left to wonder what he was really thinking.

I felt frustrated and angry as I realized that I had been mistaken about the level of our relationship. The few times we had interacted had felt so intimate, as if we could be entirely honest and open with each other, but now I realized that that wasn't the case. I was acting like a high school girl with a crush, getting ahead of myself and expecting too much too soon. I needed to take a step back and remember that the relationship was still in its early stages, and that I had to be patient and understanding. I had to remind myself that I barely knew this person, after all.

I tried to distract myself from thinking about the elephant in the room by setting up my desk and immersing myself in work. Although I still had moments of contemplation, I made a conscious effort to stay focused. I was determined not to let my emotions consume me; instead, I chose to occupy my time with productive tasks.

Whatever was going to happen next was going to happen, regardless of anything that I said or did.

And that terrified me.

Chapter 15

♥

Randy

To say that there was a monkey on my back would not have described the feeling that I had tugging at my heart and soul. I felt like a heavy weight was pressing down on my chest, a black hole of guilt in my stomach. I hated lying to Madison, as she was the one person I promised to always be honest with. She made me so happy, and I felt like I was taking that for granted by keeping this secret from her. But I couldn't bring myself to tell her that she was naked on the internet.

I created a series of lies to convince myself that it was okay to deceive her. I told myself that no one would ever find out, that she wouldn't be hurt by the truth, and that she would be better off without knowing. But these were all lies; she deserved honesty, respect, and to know the truth.

But I did something else, arguably more horrible. As I rewatched the footage, I felt a deep sense of guilt and shame. I had done something so wrong, so incredibly wrong. I had allowed my carnal desires to take over and I had masturbated to the sight of her on the security camera. She was so beautiful and so sexy that I couldn't help myself. Seeing her emotions play out all over again in a different angle was a glorious and powerful experience, one that I will never forget. She was the epitome of what every man dreams of, and I was lucky enough to experience it. Her curves, her nipples, her exquisite beauty; it was all too much for me to resist. As I felt her presence around me in that moment, I realized how much I loved her and how much she meant to me. The whole experience changed my perspective and I was forever grateful for it.

That night, I sat there, my hard cock in my hand, and my fingers running along the veins. I knew I had to do something drastic to make up for my bad behavior. I had taken her out of work and to a private island, and then I had sex with her in the workplace. I had also pushed her into becoming an online pornstar without her knowing. I was a terrible influence. I was not the kind of person who should be around her. I knew that my punishment had to be severe if I was ever going to feel okay about myself again. Oh, how I hated myself.

The following day, Madison and I worked in an uncomfortable silence. I felt like I was on stage, struggling to remember my lines. I was so overwhelmed by the secret I kept from her that I could hardly concentrate. Every time I looked at her, my anxiety rose. I was not used to keeping secrets, and it weighed heavily on me. I could hardly bear the tension in the air.

"I know I told you I wouldn't pry anymore. But, Randy, something is seriously off. We no longer hang out. You barely talk to me at work. You barely look at me. What am I supposed to think right now? Is there some other girl?"

"No— no, Madison. Absolutely not." I knew I shouldn't respond if she asked why I was acting strange, but I couldn't let her think I'd been with another woman. I had more integrity than that.

"Okay, then what is it, Randy? I'm really struggling with this; it's really driving me crazy. Leaving work every day with this feeling of uncertainty and feeling like I haven't done enough is really taking a toll on me. Is this really it, Randy? Are we really over?"

I felt like I should have been asking her that question, but I hadn't yet. I knew that I would ask her once the news came out, if it ever did. I finally said, "We're not through. Not by a long shot. I want you in my life."

"Are you telling me that you want me in your life, but not romantically? I'm not naive, I know when someone isn't interested anymore. I keep telling myself that I'm not stupid and I wasn't born yesterday, and it's not fair to me. What's going on?"

The tension in my chest was overwhelming; I was about to lose my temper. I didn't want to snap at her; she didn't deserve that. Well, she didn't deserve a lot of things. Her privacy being violated by having her nude body shared online is at the top of that list.

As she sat there waiting for me to respond, no words came out of my mouth. I was at a loss for what to say. I wanted to explain the situation to her, but I knew I couldn't without causing her more pain. So I sat in silence, unable to find the right words to say.

"I'm going to grab a coffee," I said, already out of my seat.

"That's it? You're just going to walk out like that? We're not going to finish this discussion?"

Don't snap. Don't snap. *Don't snap*. I kept saying it over and over in my head. I knew I wasn't myself at that moment. Anyone would snap after being forced to talk. I kept my cool.

"Madison, we are at work. There's nothing to talk about here."

I swiftly exited the office and firmly shut the door behind me before she could say another word.

That felt fitting, as I sensed she was about to shut the door on me, too

Some things were just inevitable.

Chapter 16

♥

Madison

It was a Friday afternoon, signaling the start of the weekend. With some free time ahead of us, I entertained the thought of Randy and I hanging out like before. But I quickly dismissed the thought, knowing it was foolish.

There were four coworkers in the office, barely talking to one another. Now granted, there were times when Randy seemed to change his tune. Every now and then he would try to start a conversation as if things were normal. But then it went right back to him being squirmish, silent, and everything in between. I honestly didn't know what to make of it. I had stopped formulating different plot lines in my head. At that point, there was no way that I could even come up with the truth. Because at that point it felt like the truth would be so far-fetched that I couldn't even come close to what it actually was.

I was confused. We had been getting along, but suddenly it felt like we were sitting at two desks that were miles apart. Every time I attempted to figure out what was happening, he would go and get coffee or take a phone call, or simply ignore me. I was beginning to wonder if we had broken up. It felt like the upcoming weekend would determine the answer.

I was confused when he didn't ask me out. I thought maybe he was uncomfortable with breaking up since we worked together. When I asked him if we were still together, he said yes. This left me feeling confused and frustrated. I knew I wasn't imagining things, I wasn't going crazy. I knew that if anyone else was in my situation they would have felt the same way. The whole situation made no sense and left me feeling baffled.

On that Friday afternoon, my gaze kept on returning to the clock while I tried to focus on the handsome Randy seated across from me. His eyes would meet mine every now and then, yet he never managed to crack a smile. He didn't even bother asking me out or inquire about my plans for the night. His lack of interest in me was almost palpable, and I felt like I had become unappealing. It felt strange to go from being admired to being ignored, but that was how it felt.

I was tempted to ask him what he was doing for the weekend, but I decided against it. We had had a difficult week and he didn't deserve to get anything out of me. Screw that. And you know what? Screw the job, too.

"Since it's Friday and I got all my work done, I think I'm going to head home. I don't feel great," I blurted out.

He was so deep in thought that he was startled when the silence was broken.

At that moment, I suddenly thought he might say something to turn the situation around. However, he simply said, "All right Madison. Have a good weekend."

Those words felt like a punch in the gut. Usually, they're the best thing to hear at the end of the week. But instead of being excited for a weekend of fun, I was just filled with dread. *Have a good weekend?* Those three words felt like a heavy weight on my shoulders.

I couldn't bring myself to let him see any of what I was feeling. He didn't deserve to see any of it.

So instead of saying something like, "you too," I silently turned my back on him and left the office.

As I walked across the work floor, the sound of keyboards clacking and conversations between coworkers filled the air. It felt like I had been released from prison. The office that I had once worked in was now a metaphorical hell hole that was a stark contrast to the moments I had spent with him in the past. Change can be difficult to accept, yet it can happen in the blink of an eye. I sighed as I realized this and began to resent the ever-changing world around me.

I pressed the down button on the elevator, and the door opened almost instantly. My life felt like it was headed in the same direction—downward. It was strange to think that Randy, the man who had changed my life in such a dramatic way, had become my poison.

Regardless of how hurt I was, all I could do was put a mask on... *Metaphorically,* that is.

Chapter 17

♥

Randy

I knew I had done wrong by Madison and that's why I was scared of our relationship ending. I had been pushing her away with my secret and it had taken its toll. She had stopped texting me. I didn't want things to end between us, but I knew it was my fault and that I deserved everything she was doing.

I found myself at a bar with a friend of mine, James. We didn't work at the same company or anything; we had just been friends since college.

No matter how much our lives changed or how much money we amassed, our friendship remained the same. We never once lost touch, so it was a comfort that I could be my authentic self around him and never feel the need to put on any sort of act.

"You really don't seem like yourself man. For as long as I've known you, you've never been this inside your head. That girl really got you trippin,'" James said to me before sipping his whiskey.

I had to tell someone; it wasn't like no one knew about what was on my mind. "Yeah well, I gotta tell you something, man."

"You already know you can tell me anything," he reassured me.

"Madison and I had sex in the office," I spat out.

"Hey, congrats," he gave me a slap on the back, almost causing me to spill my drink.

"There's a catch: there was a camera in the office and some footage got leaked." As I said this,

James' eyes widened. " She doesn't know about the footage, and, honestly, I don't know what to do. I can't bring it to myself to tell her."

He put down his glass and looked at me like I was a half-wit. "Randy, how long has this been going on?"

"A week or so."

Randy's face shifted from one of disbelief to shock, and it was just the reality check I needed. "Randy, you can't keep this from her for this long. It doesn't matter if it's a guy or a girl, no one likes their intimate moments exposed online. Every second you don't tell her is a betrayal. You may have dated many women before, but relationships are different. She won't be happy about this."

I knew all this from my own experience with relationships, and I wanted him to understand the gravity of the situation. I needed to tell her the truth, and soon, before it was too late.

My throat went dry at the thought. It was hard to sit in the office and remain silent, without being able to put an end to our situation. But the thought of her being truly angry with me filled me with fear. I didn't want to lose her. Despite only knowing her for a short time, I wanted a future with her. It was a crazy thought, but it was true.

"You look like you've seen a ghost," James said.

"Because I'm realizing that I really screwed up. The one thing that I told this woman was that I was a *changed* man. I told her that she could trust me. I had her trust in my hands and I dropped it like some sort of glass ball," I said, taking another swig of my Roy Rogers. "I was doing so well, and now it's all done. I'm going to tell her this and she's going to hate my guts."

"Don't you think that you're jumping the conclusions just a little bit? I'm going to go out on a limb here. If this girl gave you a chance—right?—and she let you into her life after not trusting you, then it's not going to be easy for her to lose that trust. This isn't the worst thing that you could do. Hell, keeping it from her will probably be what she's more angry about"

"You don't know this woman, James. She is unwavering in her beliefs and convictions. We started off on the wrong foot and it seems like that's still the case. I'm determined to make this work, but judging by your face, I know I'm in for a challenge."

James took another sip of his whiskey, emptying the bottle. "Well, I hope you figure it out. Because as long as I've known you, I've never seen you this happy... you know, apart from the circumstances."

"How can you tell while I'm mortified?"

"Hey, I know you're probably feeling scared and like you're going to mess up, but I can see how bad you want this. That's happiness, man. All these jitters and anxious feelings in your chest?

That's happiness too. You actually care about a woman. That's saying a lot. So, if I were you, I'd do whatever it takes to save her. But, maybe work on saving yourself first."

That night, I went home and followed James' advice. I put away my phone, turned off the TV, and cleared my head of anything that would distract me from what needed to be done the next day: telling Madison the truth. I knew it was going to be difficult and painful, but I also knew it was the right thing to do. As James had said, she deserves nothing less. I was ready to face the consequences of my actions, no matter the outcome.

I was no longer afraid. It was going to happen.

The next day was nerve-wracking. Nothing felt normal. I spilled my coffee and was late, but the worst part was that Madison hadn't arrived. Her desk was empty and she hadn't called out. Was this her way of putting in her resignation? I hoped not, because I'd come so close to making things right and hadn't. That wouldn't have been satisfying.

I waited with bated breath for her to walk through the door and give me a second chance.

...

A third technically, but who's counting?

Chapter 18

Madison

The man's name was Henry. Henry, Head of Security. Seeing what he had pulled up on the screen mortified me. My stomach churned as he quickly turned away, as though he hadn't already seen it. The only positive thing about the whole situation was his attempt to spare me from having to look at it.

Henry's role did not matter, to put it bluntly. He was merely a piece of the puzzle that helped me realize what I needed to know: Randy had claimed to have erased the security office's footage, but he had overlooked certain databases.

"You know, you're on a few websites too." Henry added.

My heart had nearly stopped. I felt like I couldn't breathe. How could my bare ass be on not one, but a few websites? I would never have wanted to even show it on a security camera, let alone the internet. It was like the most intimate thing a woman could do, besides putting in a tampon or taking a really bad dump. Maybe even jerking off was up there on the list. But thankfully, I hadn't done that.

"Are you okay?" he asked.

Okay was a long shot from what I was.

I felt a complicated mix of emotions after discovering my private footage had been released online without my knowledge. I felt broken, embarrassed, ashamed, and most of all betrayed.

I had trusted Randy, the person who had released the footage, to keep it private, and his failure to do so caused me pain. So yeah, no words in the dictionary could accurately describe the hurt I was feeling; it was unique. I could work to get the footage removed, but I could not erase the fact that Randy had not told me.

"I'm peachy, Henry. Thank you for showing me this. Can you please do everything in your power to remove this footage?"

"Yes ma'am. I just had this feeling that you should see it with your own eyes."

For a moment, I felt a connection to Henry. He clearly wanted to show me it without Randy's knowledge. "Thank you. I really appreciate it."

My eyes burned with rage as I stormed away from Henry, my fists clenched and my entire body filled with adrenaline. It was still early morning, yet my anger was so intense I felt like I had been transported back to my infancy. I walked faster and faster, eager to reach the office and express my anger to Randy. Hopefully, my rage would dissipate soon, and I could move past this episode.

I pretty much kicked the door open. Then I slammed it behind me. Randy's stupid little head jolted up to look at me.

Before he could even blink, I said in what became a sort of crescendo, ""You lied to me. You didn't tell me what was going on. You say you've changed, but how am I supposed to see that when you do something like this? What do you call this, Randy?"

"I take it you've seen the footage."

"You said you were going to have it taken care of. I don't care if it was a mistake. I don't care if you did this on purpose. *You didn't tell me.*" I felt my eyes starting to water. “And that's what hurts the most: the fact that you kept this from me.You know how I feel about honesty and transparency. Is that why you've been so closed off? Is that why you haven't been talking to me this week? You make me feel like I'm nothing with your lack of emotion. Do you even care how *I* feel? Don't you—"

"That's not true, Madison. The whole reason that I was acting this way all week is because I felt terrible—"

"—Shut up Randy! I'm not done speaking. You have no idea what it feels like to realize that our sex tape is on the web."

"I can have my legal team take it—"

"Randy! I'm. Not. Done. Speaking. T

I'm done. This is it. You've shown me that you don't care about how I feel or what I go through. I'm hurt and I can't take it anymore. So I'm breaking up with you. Don't bother trying to talk me out of it. I'm done."

Without looking at him, I opened the door and left.

It was a painful breakup. I had to leave a job that had been paying my bills for so long, and I was devastated. My nest egg was a comfort, but it didn't stop the heartache. I felt so small and powerless. I felt like all of the walls I had so carefully built up around myself had been smashed to pieces, and all that was left was a pile of bricks. I was firmly behind the wall again, and it would be a long time before I trusted anyone else.

Randy may have made me feel good in the moment, as if I was escaping reality and discovering that the world could be unpredictable in a positive way, almost like a fairytale. After that, I no longer had any interest in romance.

Frankly, he killed romance for me. Romance and trust. God, how I regret going to that ball.

If he's CEO of anything, it's being a dick.

Ha! *Skydick.*

Chapter 19

♥

Randy

I worked overtime that night for a very important reason: to try and get rid of the sex tape that had been posted online. I called every legal team and private investigator I knew, as well as various police teams and government agencies, and reached out to other billionaires with tech savvy to see if they could help erase the video. I did everything I could to ensure that no trace of that video remained, both for the girl's sake and for my own.

I was overcome with guilt and embarrassment. It was one of the biggest blunders of my life, worse even than anything I had done while intoxicated. I questioned if I even had a chance at repairing the damage I'd done. Could I ever reach out to her again? How was I supposed to make up for such a catastrophic error? Most people had urged me to move on, and even my friend had agreed.

As the sun set, I sat in my office, feeling more isolated and alone than ever before. Despite having hundreds of followers on social media, I was completely alone in my ivory tower. The one person I wanted to be there with me was completely out of reach, and I felt a deep sadness as I watched the sun dip below the horizon.

I rummaged through my desk, my fingers eventually finding the whiskey bottle. I knew that one crack of the bottle and one pour of the glass would be enough to undo all the sobriety I had built up over the past months.

I got out the glass next and stared at it, feeling a twinge of sadness. I had made such huge strides in my sobriety over the past few months and yet here I was, considering throwing it all away. It was like I was punishing myself, and it felt wrong. Then I thought back to when I first had my own business. I was so hard on myself, telling myself it was too small. But I'd made so much progress! I was proud of myself for that. Ultimately, there was one thing that was stopping me from opening that bottle and drinking it.

Madison.

Sure, Madison hated my guts. She wanted nothing to do with me. But I did know one thing: the girl did not want me to relapse.

I knew I had to do something drastic to stop myself from drinking the whiskey, so I put the bottle and glass away and punched the wall. I knew it wasn't the best decision, but it was necessary and it ended up helping me more than it would have if I did it for someone else.

The wall before me was a formidable presence. Its industrial concrete was cold and unyielding. My hand felt as though it might be broken, though I couldn't be sure. My real injury was in my mind. It was too worn out to express what I was feeling in my heart, but my brain was a mess. I needed a plan to get Madison back. How could I do it?

I paced the office, my nerves getting the better of me. I eyed my desk, where the whiskey bottle sat, and thought about it longingly. James had been right -- I liked Madison more than I'd let on. But how do you make someone love you again, especially after the leak of a sex tape? I had no idea.

I asked a pastor at a church located a block away from my workplace what his thoughts on the matter were.

"It sounds like you're desperate for this woman's love."

"I am. I'd do anything to get her back. But I have no idea how to. God, I can't remember the last time I even stepped foot in the church, but I'm completely at my wit's end."

"It's a very foul thing that you did. Very indecent yes," he criticized me, but it was warranted. " If you want to rebuild trust with her, you need to demonstrate that you understand the magnitude of what you did and take responsibility for it. Show her that you are committed to making things right and that you want to make sure she feels safe and secure. Ask her what else she is struggling with in the aftermath of the video being leaked, and listen to her with empathy and understanding. What is it that *you* think is still plaguing her besides the fact that you didn't tell her about that awful tape being leaked?"

"I don't know. I guess I also feel bad about the fact that no one knows that we're dating. And if anyone does know it's because of that tape."

“Instead of parading your relationship with your partner around for the world to see, you’re relationship has been made public through a sex tape. This is an incredibly embarrassing situation for your partner—and you as well, I’m sure— and it makes it difficult for her to trust you when you keep your relationship a secret.”

"Holy shit." I said.

The pastor looked mortified.

"I apologize for my language, Father. Your words have truly inspired me and filled me with a newfound appreciation. I am truly grateful for your guidance. Thank you, really.”

He smiled. "I don't know what I did but you're welcome sir."

I knew there was no guarantee, but I had to take a chance and try to fix things.

Chapter 20

♥

Madison

I woke up and stared at the ceiling for a moment, feeling a sense of freedom that I had never felt before. I had just quit my job, and while the lack of a paycheck was a bit nerve-wracking, I was excited at the prospect of what I could do with my newfound free time. I had even started a porn career, though I had no intention of pursuing it seriously. It was a joke I liked to make with my friends, a way of self-medicating through self-deprecation. Even if it sometimes led to tears at the end of the day.

I forced myself out of bed and made my breakfast. After quitting my job, I felt like I was stuck in a rut each morning. The bed was so inviting, and I didn't have to worry about anything at all. No thoughts of sex tapes or Randy entered my mind while I was comfortable and relaxed. But I knew I had to be productive and figure out how to pay my bills. I decided to get out of bed and start my day, even though I wanted to stay in the warm, cozy bed.

I made my way out of bed, feeling the chill of the floorboards beneath my feet. Taking a deep breath, I stretched my limbs and allowed my hunger to set in. I knew that breakfast was the perfect way to start the day with a sense of comfort, and I wasn't going to let my worries get in the way of that. Bacon and eggs were my go-to; the warmth of the food helped to ease my mind, even though my world felt like it was consumed by flames.

As I descended the stairs to my kitchen, I reminded myself that I wasn't the first woman to have a sex tape leaked. In fact, many women had gone on to have successful careers despite it. Life was unpredictable, and I couldn't be sure what the outcome would be. Taking out the eggs and bacon, I switched on the kitchen TV.

The kitchen TV was a habit I picked up from my mom's generation. Back then, having a TV in the kitchen was commonplace. Even though I never adopted the gaudy decor of that era, the TV remained. It made me feel at home, like the warmth of eggs and bacon. When everything went downhill, I wished I had called my mom. She would have been a comforting ear, unlike my friends who were supportive but couldn't provide the motherly love I was looking for.

In any case, I flipped on the TV and got my breakfast ready.

"We interrupt this program for a special announcement from the Mayor."

I stopped to watch whatever had been interrupted on the television. Mayor Gotch appeared on the screen, standing at a podium in the city hall. I noticed the fancy banners hung in the back and wondered if we were about to go into some sort of nuclear Cold War. With all the strange turns my life had been taking lately, I wouldn't be surprised if that were the case. Anything seemed possible at that point. I had learned to expect the unexpected.

"Good morning everyone, I have a very unorthodox meeting today. I called this press conference for a friend of a very long time. Mutual friends with billionaire James Camry," he spoke carefully. "I understand that I should not be doing this as mayor, but I owe the man a favor, and I am one to keep my word. With that said, I'm going to turn this podium over to Randy Maven."

I dropped my spatula on the floor, sending little specks of scrambled eggs everywhere; I barely noticed the mess.

"Ladies, gentlemen," he greeted everyone. "As Mayor Gotch here has introduced me, I'm Randy Maven. And I'm here today to speak about the love of my life." He cleared his throat. "I know that if I send a text, I will receive no response. A call, same result. Knocking on her door? I'd be met with no answer." He rubbed his forehead. "And this is because I did something very bad: I betrayed her trust. I kept a secret from her. Keeping that secret, as it turned out, was indeed worse than the secret itself. I mean, the actual secret was pretty bad too but—" his voice trailed off. "This woman has turned my life around in the most miraculous of ways. She challenged me to grow and pushed me outside of my comfort zone. I was scared of her because I knew she wouldn't stand for anything less than my best, but in hindsight, I'm so grateful she held me to such a high standard. I never wanted to disappoint her, so when I made a mistake, I kept it a secret. But today, it's time to throw off the mask and shout it out: I love you! Your unwavering strength and resilience has been an inspiration to me, and I will forever be grateful for the impact you've had on my life."

By the time I had processed it all, my bacon was cold.

Chapter 21

♥

Randy

My brave feat had been broadcast across town, and it quickly went viral. Everywhere I looked, women of all ages were talking about me. But I didn't do it to become an overnight sensation, I did it for one person—Madison. I had to get her back. Nothing else mattered.

The hardest part about that whole experience wasn't standing up and humbling myself in front of the world, it was the fact that she didn't respond afterwards. The one person I wanted to reach, I couldn't seem to get through to. I don't know if she saw it or if it had any effect on her, but all my efforts seemed to be in vain.

My heart sank as I sat at my desk the day after the press conference. I had hoped to hear from her, even just a thank you, but the lack of communication only deepened my disappointment, frustration, and sadness.

I couldn't concentrate on anything that day. My mind was filled with a sense of anxiety and self-doubt that I hadn't felt since I was a teenager asking a girl out for the first time. I was struggling to string together a complete sentence in meetings and my emails were a mess. It was so overwhelming that I just wanted to escape my body and run away.

There was a knock on my office door and Bradley from Human Resources had arrived. Based on our past experiences together, I knew this meeting was not going to bring any good news. I wasn't particularly fond of Bradley, but I had to maintain professionalism in the workplace. This time, however, I was in no position to be a mediator or to side with anyone. Instead, I just wanted to tell him to leave and not bother me with any more of his trivial human resource issues.

"Hey boss, just wanted to let you know you have a guest here. Former employee."

I felt my stomach churn as I heard the door opening, signaling that visitors had arrived. I groaned inwardly, recognizing that it was likely one of the former employees who had left the company years ago and had returned, hoping for a handout from me. "Who is it?" I asked Bradley, my assistant, before allowing them in. "Let me see if I can remember them first."

Bradley smiled. "I don't think you'll have a problem recognizing her," he said.

As soon as she opened the door, Madison stepped inside and shut it behind her. She then proceeded to take a seat at my desk. I was speechless."

"I didn't think you were going to— I didn't think I'd ever see you again."

"All you have to do is type 'CEO and secretary' into Pornhub, and then you get to see me all you want."

Although I appreciated the humor of the joke, I could not bring myself to laugh. "The tape is off the internet. I had everyone under the sun—"

"I'm joking with you, Randy. Did you lose your sense of humor overnight?"

I let out a sigh. "When I thought that I was losing you, yeah, I did lose my sense of humor. It's been nothing to laugh about."

She smiled coyly. "It's really sweet of you that you care so much. But you don't have to worry about losing me again," she said, and I could hardly believe my ears. "I forgive you."

Once more, it felt like I was dreaming. I had to remind myself that this was actually happening. "Thank you Madison," I said, before quickly adding, "But what does forgiveness entail? Of course I want you in my life. But I also want you as my girlfriend. Because I love you."

"Well I'll say this—"

My heart plummeted. She was rejecting me. She was walking away. And she was doing it in the most courteous manner she could manage.

"I love you too. That should answer your question as to whether or not I'll be your girlfriend."

My face lit up like a Christmas tree right after Thanksgiving when I heard the words. I couldn't believe it! I leapt up from my chair and leaned over the desk to give her a kiss.

That evening, I took her to the boardwalk, a place for us to be undisturbed and free from worldly distractions. We watched the sun sink below the horizon, the sky adorned with a beautiful sunset. I was struck by how much more special it was to share the moment with someone I loved. Having that special connection with another person makes the world a brighter place.

I stopped walking, my heart filled with emotion at her words. I leaned in and kissed her. It was a long, passionate kiss, one that promised our souls would find each other in the moments that followed. Our tongues intertwined, our bodies becoming one.

"I promise you, if I ever lie to you ag—"

She kissed me so as to shut me up. And I was okay with that. Because I, too, was tired of talking. I'd much prefer sex.

Chapter 22

♥

Madison

Love is complicated and doesn't come without its own unique set of challenges. It's often romanticized in movies and songs, but in reality, it's much more complex than that. When you're in a relationship, you open yourself up to the possibility of getting your heart broken. It can be the most frightening thing ever, as there is no protection or shield between you and your partner. You become vulnerable and put all your feelings out there. The walls that once existed between two people are now gone.

I was filled with a euphoric sense of liberation when I finally got rid of the metaphorical bricks in my life. With nothing holding me back, I opened up to Randy and felt a deep trust in him, despite meeting him when we wore only masks. As I lay on his bed and we kissed passionately, I felt a sense of security and knew that he was the one for me.

My hand was resting on his hip as I felt the warmth of his skin against my fingertips. His chest was bare, and the sight of his chest hair was tantalizing. I felt my desire growing with each passing second, and I could feel my body becoming increasingly aroused.

I wasn't a shallow person, but I couldn't believe my luck with Randy. His body was incredibly chiseled, despite only working out twice a week, and his features were like something out of a GQ magazine. There were times when I felt like

I was out of his league—I wasn't one to be easily impressed by looks, but he was certainly something special.

His hand moved to my breast and gave it a gentle squeeze. The second squeeze was a little firmer, as if he was trying to convey his hunger for me. I found this incredibly arousing, and I wanted him to want me and take me. Knowing that he loved me and desired me made me feel incredibly close to him. With all my walls down, I felt completely vulnerable to him and it was the most amazing feeling.

He suddenly stopped lying next to me, and before I could comprehend what was happening, he had climbed on top of me. His hands grabbed the hem of my tank top and pulled it up, revealing my bare breasts to him. His eyes were wide with excitement, almost like he had just uncovered a hidden treasure. He then leaned in and began to suck on one of my nipples, hard. His actions reminded me of a lion enjoying its feast.

Randy's hand slipped lower, sending waves of pleasure through me as he touched my clit. His touch was different from anyone else's, rougher and more confident. He knew exactly how I liked it, and it was a reminder that he really cared about me. I never thought something so intimate could also be a sign of genuine affection, but it was true. His attentiveness in the bedroom was a reflection of how attentive he was in all aspects of our relationship.

He removed my underwear and held me more firmly. He then placed his hand over my vulva, gently tapping it. When I began to climax, I had to move his hand away, to which he chuckled.

"Don't laugh; I can't help it. You're good at what you do."

"Only when it comes to you, baby."

He once again disappeared from view and I felt my legs being spread wide open. Though I had already exposed myself to him in the past, this position felt particularly vulnerable. I reminded myself that he had already seen me in every way possible, but I couldn't help but feel exposed as he looked directly into my most intimate area.

I was lost in a sea of pleasure from the way his tongue danced around my most sensitive areas. His expert tongue found all the right places, making me wetter and more aroused with every second. I could feel myself getting closer and closer to climaxing, but all I wanted was for him to take me, to feel the fullness of his manhood deep inside me. I wanted it to fill me up, to make me feel like I was full of him. Every time he made love to me, it felt like he was going deeper and deeper, and I wanted to experience that feeling again. His size was always a pleasant surprise, and I wanted to feel that pleasure once more.

I watched his head bob up and down between my legs, only his eyebrows visible at one point. His multitasking was remarkable as he probed my depths with two fingers while his tongue worked its magic on my clit. His every action seemed to be simultaneously pleasurable for both of us.

"Oh my god yes." I blurted out. "You're so good. Oh my God. Keep going, just like that. Yes! Yes, baby, yes!"

He did really well by maintaining the same pace despite my comments; this forced me to push his head away from my crotch.

"Got her again," he said proudly.

"I just don't want to come that way. Put it on me."

"Can you suck it first?"

I grinned with delight, eager to take his cock into my mouth.

I laid him down on the bed, undoing his pants to reveal his hard, veiny penis. I was a bit intimidated, unsure if I'd be able to accommodate him. But, I decided to give it my best shot and took his member in my mouth. I was determined not to let him down after all the pleasure he had given me.

I was totally immersed in the sensation. Every detail of his cock was clear to me, from the ridges to the bumps. It was like being in a car and driving over a bumpy road. I felt each and every bump carefully as I observed them all. I was paying close attention, and the experience was deeply satisfying.

I took pleasure in the way my lips reached the very top of his pubic hair. It almost seemed like I could fit his entire cock in my mouth. In the end, it was he who had to lift my head off of him. I looked up with a smile and asked, "What happened?"

"Quiet down, Madison. Don't get cocky."

I glanced downward at his groin, him not realizing the pun he had just made.

As I was about to respond, he stopped my sarcasm in its tracks; his hands on my body as he laid me down. His hard cock pushing inside of me felt like I'd been waiting for forever. He filled me up completely and all I could do was melt into the bed beneath us. I watched his face, pleasure washing over him as he moved in and out of me. Gone was the masquerade mask from years ago, and in its place, the love and connection we'd built up over time. I didn't have to wait long before I felt my orgasm take over, and I was grateful for the journey that had brought us to this moment.

We lay naked, cuddled up on the bed. His body was my island of serenity, providing me with the calmness I had felt when we had gone away together. I draped my leg over his and sighed contentedly. "I wish we could go back there," I murmured.

"To where?" he asked.

"That island you took me to. I really loved it. It was like no place I had ever been. And it reminds me of you. It reminds me of a time where everything was simple."

"That was also the place where things... hit the fan."

"I guess. But I don't remember it like that. And when you say 'hit the fan,' I look at that situation more is you being so scared to tell me something that could hurt me. And that means the world to me, Randy. I really love you."

He looked at me with a glossy expression, and it seemed like he was getting emotional. "Madison, you have no idea how much I love you," he said.

Love is a complex thing. It can make you feel vulnerable and scared all at the same time. But despite that, I wouldn't trade it for anything else.

I was so lucky to have found Randy, who showed me that love indeed exists. His love for me was evident in his eyes, and he saw something in me that I couldn't even see in myself. So when people asked me if I had a happily ever after despite my trust issues, the answer was a resounding yes. Love may be complex, but it is also beautiful and worth fighting for.

Because I **loved** Randy Maven.

Epilogue

♥

Randy

I was aware that Madison was conscious of how much I adored her. I didn't feel the need to convince her any more. But in the depths of my heart, I wanted to. Love, I learned, is a continuous journey. Once you are in it, you understand the truth. People tend to think that when you're in love, that's it, and you can stop trying. But that couldn't be further from reality. Love needs to be cultivated like a garden, requiring maintenance and care. It's almost like a business—though I didn't like to think of it this way. You can have a business, but if you don't know how to keep it running, you'll soon go bankrupt.

So what exactly did I do to sustain my love with Madison? Among the top was treating her to a trip to the little island she adored.

"I can't believe that I get to come here whenever I want to. Well, I mean whenever you bring me," she said, eyes twinkling as we watched the ocean's ebb and flow.

"Do you think you could ever get sick of a place like this?"

"You can't get sick of things that you truly love. That's like if I asked you if you would ever get sick of me."

"Oh, come on now. That's an easy answer. Of course I could get sick of you; it happens most days."

As she laughed, her cute little giggle brought a smile to my face. I was so taken by her in many ways, and I wanted to tell her how much I adore her, but words wouldn't do justice to my feelings. So, as I typically did, I stepped closer and pulled her in for a long kiss under the warm sun. My nerves started to fade away as soon as our lips met, and my heart started to beat faster as if it was dancing at a rave.

When Madison pulled off from our kiss, she looked at me with inquisitive eyes. "Why do I sense some tension?"

I shrugged. "Maybe because I'm about to do this."

I got down on one knee, struggling a bit to get the ring box out. Finally, after a few seconds, I was able to produce the box and open it up.

Madison's hands flew to her face and tears began to stream down her cheeks. I felt a wave of relief wash over me; it seemed like she was going to say yes! Despite our happy relationship, I couldn't help but feel a slight bit of anxiety about her response. I wanted her to say yes more than anything.

"Madison, I love you with all my heart and I couldn't picture myself being with anyone but you. Will you marry me?"

Before I had a chance to finish my sentence, she was already nodding in agreement and then suddenly embraced me in a hug.

I scooped her up off her feet, her hug tight around me as she began to sob. I wanted her to see the ring I had spent a fortune on, but I was happy that she didn't need to. "Hey I'm happy that you're happy," I said softly, "but take a look at the ring."

She let out her signature giggle before glancing down at the ring. Her face lit up in shock, just as he had anticipated. "It's stunning, Randy. You shouldn't have spent so much money on me."

"Of course I should have. You deserve it. Especially after everything that we've been through."

She kissed me again, her tongue slipping into my mouth. This was a clear sign that she was pleased.

"Oh my God I'm engaged. I'm engaged again. It feels so weird."

"Weird in a good way or a bad way?"

"Oh, shut up!"

I couldn't help but laugh.

I couldn't believe that I had to plan a wedding. After attending only three weddings in my entire life, two of which I was severely drunk for, I felt overwhelmed and unprepared. I had always thought that drinking at my own wedding would be a right of passage, but here I was, soberly planning out my special day.

I was so excited to marry Madison. My nerves were on edge, but I knew that when it was all said and done, we would be standing together at the altar, and I couldn't wait for that moment. After the ceremony, we would go on our honeymoon, start a life together, and possibly even become parents. Material things weren't important to me, because all I wanted was to spend my life with the beautiful Madison. She was my one and only drug and I was drunk with love for her. I was ready to embark on this journey to create our own white picket fence future.

We would don our masks one day and share a hearty laugh. We were strangers when we first met, but the bond we forged was so strong that she eventually adopted my last name.

I looked at her again, recalling the first time I ever saw her, at our masked encounter; *a literal blessing in disguise*. Her lips had been captivating since then.

Let the fresh start commence. No masks required.

www.ingramcontent.com/pod-product-compliance
Lightning Source LLC
LaVergne TN
LVHW091326150826
845673LV00006B/1791